Contents

Apollo 11

In May 1961, the US President, John F. Kennedy, made a famous speech in which he set a new national goal for America: to land a man on the Moon and return him safely to Earth by the end of the decade.

On 20th July 1969, the US space administration, NASA, achieved this goal when *Apollo 11* landed on the lunar surface. The whole world was watching as astronauts Neil Armstrong and Buzz Aldrin became the first humans to walk on the Moon. Sadly, John F. Kennedy was not there to see it. He was shot dead by an assassin in Dallas, Texas in November 1963.

CHAPTER 1
July 2019

Ryan leaped out of bed and flung open his curtains. The sky was clear and blue, as blue as the wide-open sea, broken only by a single jet trail crossing far above.

The jet's plumes streamed out behind it in straight twin lines. Ryan angled his telescope up in its direction. He peered closely at its tiny body, gleaming in the sun, as it zipped through the stratosphere. He imagined all those hundreds of people travelling aboard. Where were they going? Somewhere new and exciting – a far-off place, perhaps, with palm trees and exotic cities.

Ryan felt a rush in his heart as he thought about the day ahead, and what it would bring, for today was the day they would open the time capsule.

He flung on his school uniform and his shoes. He ducked under the models of the planets that were hanging down from the ceiling. Such was his hurry that he almost knocked over his scale model of the US Space Shuttle on his way out of the door.

Ryan heard his big sister, Martha, in her room, talking loudly, probably to one of her friends on her phone or her laptop. Ryan poked his head around the door and smiled. "Morning!"

Sure enough, Martha was at her laptop, surrounded by the books and papers that she was studying for her degree. Martha was a lot older than Ryan. She was at university. She was just about to sit her final exams. Another girl's face was shining back on the screen.

"What?" Martha twisted her head round, her glasses perched on the end of her nose. "Oh, yeah, morning. I'm on to Tanusha. It's three o'clock where she is."

Ryan smiled and backed out of the room. Martha had lots of friends living all over the world.

Downstairs, Ryan wolfed down some cereal and swallowed a few gulps of orange juice. He was in too much of a hurry to get to school to bother eating. Mum had just got back from a business trip the night before, and was busy unpacking her briefcase. Dad was quiet, lost in his thoughts and staring into the distance as he nibbled on his toast. He looked a little troubled, though Ryan hardly gave it a passing thought.

"We're opening the time capsule today," Ryan announced.

Dad gazed at him. He was still miles away, Ryan could tell, and only half listening. "Hmm ... Time capsule?"

"I told you – remember? Children at the school buried it in 1969 at the time of the _Apollo_ Moon landings. That's fifty years ago exactly. We're opening it up again today."

Dad snapped out of his daze. "Oh, yes, you did tell me. That's great, Ryan."

Mum was sitting by her case, staring down absent-mindedly at a letter that was folded in her hands. Something about Mum and Dad's behaviour nagged at Ryan – the distance and the silence. It wasn't like them. Ryan glanced from Mum to Dad, then back again. "Is anything wrong?"

Mum shook her head, then turned to him and smiled, a broad, reassuring smile. "No, everything's fine, Ryan. Don't worry."

Ryan shrugged. When people told him 'everything's fine', Ryan assumed that everything really was fine. Sometimes it wasn't and they said it anyway, but Ryan could never work out the difference. He put it behind him as he raced out of the door, for there was a lot to get excited about today.

Ryan vaulted the garden wall, as usual – gates were for pedestrians and losers. He was still chewing his toast, while tucking his shirt in at the same time.

CHAPTER 2

The year AD 1890 was carved into the stone in front of Cheam Hill School. As Ryan sprinted towards the gates, a strange thought flashed into his head, a thought about all the generations of kids who'd passed through here. Today of all days, he could sense them; could sense the ghosts of their footsteps as they raced in and out of the building.

The bell had just stopped ringing, and the pupils from his own generation were already filing inside.

"Late again, Ryan," joked the man in the orange council vest who was sweeping the street outside. Mr Deegan was an old man with grey hair and a dark, wine-coloured birthmark on his upper lip. He was always sweeping round here. This was his patch.

"Ah, no, not late, Mr Deegan," he replied. "Just in time."

Mr Deegan laughed and raised his broom in a kind of salute, which he did often, and Ryan fell in behind the other pupils.

Ryan's friend, Kayden, was already at his desk, shuffling his football trading cards, when Ryan came running into the classroom. With his thick messy hair and ruffled shirt, he looked almost as untidy as Ryan did. Kayden glanced up at Ryan, caught the excited expression on his face and laughed. "Ha! Your face, Ryan. You're a space geek, you know that?"

"Come on! It's a time capsule! Full of things from the past. Does that not make you excited?" asked Ryan.

Kayden cut his cards, and sighed. "Football is exciting. Not a boring old box from the past."

Ryan's teacher, Mrs Pace, called the class to order. As the lesson began, Ryan could hardly concentrate. He fidgeted and drummed his fingers on the desk. All he could think about was the time capsule. What would it be like, and what would they find inside it?

It seemed like an age before the bell rang again, and the time came. Mrs Pace led the whole class outside to the grassy stretch around the side of the building. The air was warm and muggy. The rest of the school was filing out too, but they lined up behind. It was Ryan's class, Class 6A, that took pride of place at the front – and for a good reason. The class who buried the time capsule fifty years ago were also Class 6A.

A large boulder used to mark the spot where the time capsule was buried, but the spot was bare now. The boulder had been shifted. In its place were two shovels sticking out of the earth. A pair of council workmen in overalls stood waiting, their arms folded.

The headteacher, Mr Ferris, marched to the front. Ryan, standing at the end of a line, caught a flash of colour at the corner of his eye, something from beyond the other side of the school fence. He turned, glimpsing Mr Deegan, or at least his face, half-hidden behind bushes and peering in. *Peering sadly*, he thought. Mr Deegan half-caught Ryan's eye. Ryan smiled and waved, expecting his usual friendly wave in return. But Mr Deegan didn't wave back. He cast his eyes down and ducked out of sight, which was a bit strange, Ryan thought. Then the headteacher coughed and began to speak.

"Class 6A," he said in his booming voice. "Fifty years ago, Class 6A of Cheam Hill School buried a time capsule. The time has come for us to open it up and see what they've left us."

Mr Ferris nodded at the workmen, who spat on their hands, snatched up their spades and began to dig.

As the men worked, slowly and steadily, silence hung thick in the air. The only sounds were the gravelly crunch of the spades in the ground, then the sprinkling of the earth as they cast it behind them. Everybody watched and waited, holding their breath.

Finally, one of the spades struck something solid. One workman, the older of the two, kneeled down in the hole they'd dug and scraped away some dirt.

The man glanced up at the headteacher and nodded. "Found it."

Mr Ferris leaned over the hole to watch as the two men uncovered something, then prised it free. With a tug and a heave, out it came, a dirt-covered stainless-steel canister. At first glance, it looked like a kind of milk churn that they used to use in the old days.

The men lugged it over to a trestle table that was set up nearby. They lowered the canister on to the table top. The older workman unscrewed the cap with a twist, but he stopped short of opening it fully. He stepped back, leaving the headteacher to unscrew it the rest of the way.

Ryan wasn't sure what to expect as the cap came off: a pop, a hiss, a rush of air as the long-pent-up gases escaped? But there was nothing, just a soft click.

CLASS 6A-1969

13

CHAPTER 3

Mr Ferris reached his arm inside the time capsule.
Slowly, carefully, he lifted out a batch of envelopes –
envelopes that were small, crisp and greyish, and tied up
with string. He placed them to one side, then reached his
arm in again and began pulling out some more things.
First, a rolled-up copy of *The Times* newspaper from
the day of the *Apollo 11* landing. The headline read:
MAN LANDS ON MOON. Then he pulled out a comic,
a school tie, scarf and badge, a menu from the school
canteen, and a few smaller items.

The headteacher beckoned the class towards the table.
"Come forward and see." The class gathered round.
Kayden and some of the others clustered around a set
of old football cards. A few were interested in the comic.
One or two of the kids were laughing at the school
dinner menu and its stodgy food.

"What's bread and butter pudding?" they asked each
other.

Lastly, Mr Ferris flicked open a scrolled-up, hand-written
letter, then read it out.

To Whom it May Concern

I bring you good wishes from the year 1969!

This capsule was buried to mark the landing of human beings on the Moon. We sincerely hope this magnificent endeavour will be for the greater benefit of all humankind.

Included in this capsule, you will find letters from all the children of Class 6A to their fellow students in fifty years' time. I asked them to think about what life will be like in the future, and how it will differ from their own life now. I include a class photo so that your pupils can see the faces of the children who sent the letters.

We hope that you are lucky enough to live in a peaceful world and that your lives are happy and productive.

Yours sincerely

Miss Bradbury (Class Teacher)

And Class 6A, Cheam Hill School

Mr Ferris held the class photo in the air and showed it around, though Ryan didn't get a clear look at any of the faces. Then he untied the batch of letters.

"Take a letter each, everyone. Go and read it!" Mr Ferris began doling the letters out to the class. Ryan was so excited he wanted to barge his way to the front to get one, but somehow he managed to hold himself back, waiting in the queue like everyone else.

Finally, at the front, it was all he could do to stop himself snatching the letter out of Mr Ferris's hand. As soon as he had the letter he darted out of the crowd with it.

Ryan flopped down on a grassy bank nearby. The summer sun was peeking out from behind fluffy, white clouds. Ryan stared at the envelope, which was blank and slightly crusty under his fingertips. There was a strange, metallic taste on the tip of his tongue as he built himself up to opening it. *What was that*, he thought – *the taste of excitement?*

Kayden plonked himself down next to Ryan. He had already opened his letter, and he was laughing. "Listen to this. This guy here …" Kayden waved the letter around, "… he says that in fifty years' time humans will

have two heads because of the nuclear radiation from all the atomic wars. But it's okay, because by then we'll have flying cars." Kayden laughed again, staring down at his letter. "I like this guy. His name's John."

Ryan laughed too. He liked Kayden. It was a pity he was moving to another school at the end of term.

"When you leave Cheam Hill, will you miss me?" he asked.

"What, miss sitting next to you, listening to you talk about space all day? No chance." Kayden winked, but then looked away sadly. After a moment's pause, he nodded down at Ryan's envelope. "You not opening yours?"

Ryan turned the envelope over in his fingers. He was delaying the moment, mainly because he'd been looking forward to it so much. There was no better feeling than the feeling of looking forward to something. Now he flipped open the flap and pulled out the folded letter inside.

CHAPTER 4

Dear Whoever

My name is Clare. I love anything to do with space. I want to be an astronaut when I grow up. I am good at maths and physics so that should help!

The Apollo 11 Moon landing was the most exciting moment in my whole life. On the night of the landing, Dad took me to Trafalgar Square to watch it on the big screen. It was past my bedtime, but Dad said that didn't matter – this was too important to miss.

The atmosphere was terrific. I stood right in the middle of the square and soaked up every last detail! I didn't want to miss a thing.

Miss Bradbury has asked for three predictions for life in fifty years' time, so here you are.

- Starman will drive a roadster into space!

- Spirit and Opportunity will come to Mars, but no people!

- A New Horizon will find its heart on Pluto!

Good luck!

From Clare Smith, Class 6A

This girl, Clare, was just as fascinated by space as Ryan was. Ryan tried to imagine what it would've been like to have witnessed the moment men landed on the Moon, to be standing right in the middle of a busy crowd in Trafalgar Square, watching the Moon landing on a big screen. How exciting would that have been?

The first time he read the girl's three predictions they seemed odd and kind of funny. He couldn't quite get his head round them, so he read them again. The second time, his heart started beating faster. And by the third time, as he pored over them in detail, hairs were standing up on the back of his neck!

Ryan gasped and thrust the letter into Kayden's hands. "Read this!"

Kayden read it through, then handed it back to him. "I prefer my letter guy," he said. "My guy was funny."

"Don't you get it?" he asked.

"Get what?" Kayden was confused.

Ryan groaned. "Those three predictions?" He pointed to the page.

"What about them? They're just silly."

"Silly? They're amazing!"

"Amazing, how?" he asked.

"AMAZING!"

Kayden snatched the letter back out of Ryan's hands and read the predictions again. "Eh? Nah, I don't get it."

"Take the first one – 'Starman will drive a roadster into space'. Well, that's brilliant for a start! A few years ago, a rocket went up into space carrying a car – a roadster in fact. A dummy dressed up in a spacesuit was strapped into the front seat. They called him 'Starman'."

Kayden's eyes widened, and he nodded. "Oh, yeah. I do remember that. I suppose that's quite good."

Ryan turned to the second prediction. "Then there's 'Spirit and Opportunity will come to Mars, but no people'. *Spirit* and *Opportunity* were the names of the two Mars rovers that NASA sent to the red planet. No people ever went to Mars, but *Spirit* and *Opportunity* did!"

"What about the last one?" asked Kayden.

"That's the best one of all! We knew hardly anything at all about Pluto, not until a few years ago when a probe arrived there. The name of the probe … was *New Horizons*."

"Yeah, but what's this about finding its heart?"

"Well, the main feature on the surface of Pluto is shaped like a big, gigantic heart. Check it out on the Internet if you like. Now do you see?"

Kayden was nodding enthusiastically. "Ah, now I do. That's pretty good."

Pretty good, thought Ryan. *It was more than that. It was more than amazing. It was spooky*. A chill ran up his spine. *How could this girl, Clare, have possibly known these things? Those predictions were too good, too exact, to be just lucky guesses.*

They sat for a moment, listening to the birdsong and watching the rest of the class as they sprawled around the grass reading their own letters.

Kayden's face screwed up in thought as he asked, "How did she do it?"

"I don't know," replied Ryan. "But I'm going to find out."

CHAPTER 5

The headteacher, Mr Ferris, was still at the table, sorting through some of the items that came out of the time capsule. Ryan ran up to him.

"Sir, Sir, look at this!"

Mr Ferris took the letter from him and glanced at it, but he didn't read the predictions. He only read the name. "Clare Smith." Mr Ferris snatched up the class photo and flipped it round. A list of names was printed on the back. "A-ha! She's the second from the right, middle row."

He handed the photo to Ryan, tapping his finger on one of the faces. "That's her."

Ryan gazed closely at a pale girl with a bob haircut. Unlike most of the others in the photo, the girl wasn't smiling. *There was nothing wrong with that*, thought Ryan. He hated smiling in photos too. It wasn't a dark expression; it was sober and thoughtful. It was almost like the girl knew that one day she'd be sharing a secret with someone. With him.

Then he wondered, *what would the girl look like now?* Would she still have a thick bob of black hair? Probably

not. Maybe she'd be old and grey instead. For all Ryan knew, she might not even be alive. She might have died many years ago. But if she hadn't died, if she still lived, then what had become of her? Did she still live nearby? Did she still remember the time capsule? If so, maybe Ryan could speak to her about her predictions.

Ryan turned to the headteacher and coughed to catch his attention. "Sir, did you manage to track down any of the children from this class?"

"We did try, Ryan," replied Mr Ferris. "We put an article in the local newspaper asking for anyone from the class to get in touch, but nobody did."

"What happened to them all?" Ryan wondered aloud.

"Who knows?" said the headteacher with a shrug. "They moved away, they moved on, they lived their lives, they forgot about the time capsule."

Just then, a photographer from the newspaper arrived, and the headteacher turned away to greet him.

Some photos were taken with the class, with Ryan and Kayden and the others holding up the letters they'd received from the pupils from the past. Ryan imagined his own thoughtful expression wasn't that much different from Clare's.

Soon after, Mrs Pace led the class back inside.

"Hand back your letters please," said the teacher, but Ryan groaned. He didn't want to hand his back. He wanted to keep it. "Could I please photocopy it?" he asked, then added, "To show my parents." It was a lie, well, maybe a tiny one. He did want to show it to them, but that wasn't the real reason he wanted it.

"Of course, Ryan," said Mrs Pace. She let Ryan copy the class photograph as well.

When Ryan got home he was dying to tell someone. He burst into Martha's room. Martha's books and papers seemed to have exploded everywhere. They were spread across her bed, and even across the floor. Martha was chatting to another one of her friends on the laptop. The face reflecting back on the screen was a smiling boy with a freckled face and red hair. Ryan thought he glimpsed a palm tree through the window behind the boy's shoulder.

Martha whisked round, annoyed, and glared at him. "What is it, Ryan? I'm on to my friend Benny. It's eleven in the morning where he is."

"Ah, sorry, just wanted to, eh … Never mind." Ryan left her to it.

Mum wasn't home, but he found Dad in the shed. He was standing at his workbench, scratching his chin and staring at his bike, which was propped upside down on top of the bench. There was a distracted look about his face.

"Dad? You all right?" he asked.

Dad snapped out of his daze and smiled. "Hello Ryan. Tell me about your day."

And he did.

CHAPTER 6

Sitting round the kitchen table, Ryan told Dad all about the opening of the time capsule. He showed him the letter, and the class photo, and then he talked about the most important part, Clare's three predictions.

"Hmm, that really is uncanny," said Dad as he stared at Clare's face.

"But how can I trace this girl?" asked Ryan. "They said they put an ad in the paper, but no one came forward.

Dad sighed, then rubbed his hand across his face. "No one at all, you say?"

"Yes, no one at all. Is that strange?"

Dad shrugged. "Fifty years is a long time. Enough for a whole lifetime. Some of them might have died. Emigrated. Moved away. Others just plain forgot."

"That's what Mr Ferris said. So there's nothing I can do?"

Dad reached over and grabbed his laptop, then flipped it open. "We can check the Internet." And so they did. Ryan felt a surge of hope as Dad typed Clare's name in

and hit 'ENTER'. The problem, as they soon discovered, was that the world is full of Smiths. And plenty of Clare Smiths too. Too many in fact, and there was no one among them who seemed like she might match the description of the Clare Smith from Class 6A.

After a fruitless search, Ryan went back to his room and flopped down on the bed. He pulled the photo out again and scanned through all the faces. He was thinking of giving up. He couldn't think of a way to track Clare down.

Then everything changed, and it was all because of a face.

A single face.

Not Clare's face. It was the face of a boy further along the second row from Clare. Ryan's heart raced. There was no mistaking it. That birthmark, that wine-coloured birthmark on the upper lip.

Mr Deegan.

The next morning, Ryan skidded his bike to a halt in front of the school fence, staring in. There was something weird about being here at the weekend. The playground was deserted, apart from a few lonely gulls wandering about, looking lost.

Mr Deegan's patch, the area where he worked sweeping the streets, was the area round the school. And it really was his patch because his home was here too, just up the street from the school building. Ryan walked his bike along the line of a long, neatly clipped hedge. He spotted Mr Deegan in his garden. He wasn't alone. A woman who looked like she might be his wife was sitting on a blanket that was spread out across the grass. She was bouncing a baby up and down on her knee. Another, older, child ran around her, laughing. Mr Deegan's grandchildren perhaps.

He soon spotted Ryan too, smiling as he came over. "Hello Ryan! Fancy seeing you here on a Saturday."

"I came to ask you something, Mr Deegan," he said.

"Oh, fire away."

"I saw you yesterday at the opening of the time capsule."

"Oh?" he said, surprised. "Erm, yes."

Ryan recalled the moment he'd caught sight of Mr Deegan the day before. It was nothing strange that he was there, outside the school, because it was where he worked. No, it was the way Mr Deegan had been skulking almost, from behind the fence. The way he'd shrunk away when he caught Ryan's eye. What Ryan couldn't work out was why.

Ryan pulled out his copy of the class photo. "Mr Deegan, is this you?" He pointed out the boy with the birthmark on his face. Up close to him now, there could be no denying it. That boy was him. Mr Deegan had been one of the class in 1969.

Judging from his eyes, he seemed to accept it too. He nodded, sadly. "Yes," he said with a sigh. "That's me."

"I don't understand. Why didn't you say anything? Why didn't you come forward?" asked Ryan. As a member of Class 6A, and the only member of that class still around, then surely Mr Deegan would have been given pride of place at the capsule's opening.

"You'd better come in," he said, propping open the garden gate. Then he spotted Ryan's dad, who was poised on his own bike at the roadside. "Is that your father?" Dad had asked to come with Ryan that morning, but Ryan made him hang back a bit so that he could speak to Mr Deegan on his own.

Ryan nodded. Mr Deegan waved at Dad, and Dad waved back. "Well, he'd better come in too," said the old man, beckoning Dad towards him.

CHAPTER 7

As the morning sun beat down in the back garden, Mr Deegan slowly eased himself into a wicker chair. Ryan sat on the seat opposite to him, sipping from a glass of squash Mrs Deegan had given him.

At the other end of the garden, Dad was talking to Mrs Deegan about her roses while the baby played on the mat and the older child toddled about on the grass.

"It's all a bit embarrassing," said Mr Deegan. "You see, my class, Class 6A, were a very bright lot. I think the Moon landing inspired them. Drove them on to great things. We had this one girl who kept talking about how nothing was impossible in life, and the Moon landing proved it."

He picked up the class photo and began picking out faces. "That boy there was Brian. He became an engineer, went on to build bridges. Next to him was Roy. He became an architect. And Sarah and Blake, who both became doctors. Pete became a professor and Naina, the one standing on the end, she ended up working for the

World Health Organization, fighting diseases in Africa. I mean, how brilliant is that?"

Still staring down at the photo, Mr Deegan broke into a broad smile. "They all did so well. I'm proud of them."

He paused to take a sip from his tea, then sighed sadly. "And me? After I left school, I fell in with a bad crowd. Got into a few fist fights. Got banged up in prison for a while. My life didn't quite match up to the others."

"Are you ashamed? Is that why you never came forward?" asked Ryan.

He nodded. "A bit. I mean, they've all gone off and travelled. Look at me, I never left my home town. They've done all these wonderful things with their lives. Me? Well, when I got out of jail I decided I would never go back. Never. Got a job as a street sweeper, and it's what I've been doing ever since. It's all I've ever done. I spent my whole life sweeping these streets."

Ryan leaned forward. "Mr Deegan, do you like your work? And your life here?"

He gazed back at Ryan for a second before his eyes lit up with pride. "Yes I do. I love it! I don't think I was cut out for all that travel and adventure. I love my home town, never wanted to leave. And I love my job. I get to be outside all day. I get to meet people, and I get to see all the lovely faces of the youngsters at the school, people like you. I never tire of that."

Mr Deegan nodded at the two infants, playing and laughing with each other on the mat. His smile got even broader. "And I've got my family around me, my grandchildren. No, life couldn't be better."

"Then what do you have to be embarrassed about?" Ryan asked.

Mr Deegan thought about this for a while. "I suppose I am the black sheep of the class. I didn't think my high-achieving classmates would want me representing them."

"So you made a mistake," said Ryan. "You paid for it, you served your time. Then you got out of prison and you fixed it."

Mr Deegan nodded. "I suppose I did. But I still don't think they'd want me to represent them."

They watched the children playing for a moment while a jet streamed across the sky high above them. Ryan stared up at it, wondering, as he always did, what wonderful, new and exciting place it was headed to. Mr Deegan smiled that gentle smile that Ryan was so used to seeing in the mornings. "Nothing is impossible, but not everyone wants to reach for it, do they? Some people are happy as they are."

Since Mr Deegan knew so much about his fellow classmates, Ryan had high hopes that he could tell him about Clare. "What about this girl?" he said, pointing out Clare's face in the photo.

"Oh, now let's see. That was Clare. Yes, she was the girl I told you about."

"The one who said nothing is impossible in life?"

"Yes."

"Do you know how I could get in touch with her?"

Mr Deegan puffed out his cheeks. "Her family moved away soon after the photo was taken. I heard somewhere that they'd gone to America, but I'm afraid that's all."

"What about one of the other classmates? Someone who might have kept in touch with Clare."

Mr Deegan shrugged. "Afraid I lost contact with them all, and many years ago."

Ryan's shoulders sagged, and he slumped back on his seat. "Aw, I really wanted to speak with her about her letter."

"I can see that," said Mr Deegan. "Well …" He leaned back in his chair and slurped his cup of tea. "I don't know if I can help, but let me think about it for you." He leaned forward, smiling. "But Clare was right. Nothing is impossible, Ryan. Nothing."

CHAPTER 8

"Oh, just a thought," said Mr Deegan as he was showing Ryan and his father to the door. "You might try our old teacher, Miss Bradbury."

"She's still alive?" Ryan asked in disbelief, wondering how old she must be.

"Yes, she's very old indeed, and last I heard she was quite ill. Probably why she couldn't come yesterday."

Ryan stared at the class photo, at the prim but pleasant face of the teacher standing at one side. He recalled Mr Ferris reading out her letter, and how positive and hopeful it sounded. Ryan wondered how old the woman would be now? Judging by her face in the picture, in her eighties at least.

Mr Deegan gave Ryan the address. It wasn't far, so he and his father cycled straight there.

The house was an old sandstone cottage with ivy growing up the walls. As Ryan marched up the drive, the gravel crunching under his feet, a tall man dressed in black appeared from the front porch.

"Excuse me, does a Miss Bradbury live here?" Ryan asked.

The man, wearing a sombre expression, removed his black top hat. "I'm afraid you're too late." Then he stepped to one side as a group of men emerged, walking slowly and bearing a wooden coffin. Only now did Ryan notice the black hearse waiting nearby.

Back home, Dad found some pictures on the Internet showing Trafalgar Square on the night of the Moon landing in 1969. The photos were of a massive crowd gathered around a big screen that was set up in front of the dome and the columns of the National Gallery. Ryan tried to imagine what the atmosphere was like there as they waited excitedly for news from the Moon. It must have been nerve-wracking, for there was no guarantee that the Moon landing would be a success.

Even thinking about it, about standing there in hope, anxiously waiting on news from space, gave Ryan a tingle in his stomach.

Later that night, after another fruitless search for Clare, Ryan sat with his father in the garden, staring up at the darkening sky, watching the stars and planets as they came out one by one. Dad pointed each one out as they appeared. "Look, there's Jupiter, there's Venus, there's the star Altair."

Ryan twiddled his toes on the grass. "Dad, what if I never track down Clare? What if I never find the answer to those predictions?"

Dad thought about this for a moment before replying. "Hmm. Hundreds of years ago, before science gave us answers, people gazed up at the stars and wondered, truly wondered. They used to think the Sun, the Moon and the stars revolved around the Earth. They used to think the Earth was flat. Now we have answers to a lot of those questions. The thing is, though, the more answers we get, the more questions come up. Right now, we know more than anyone in history about the universe, but, in a way, we know even less. I keep thinking about how big the universe is, how far it goes, does it ever end? Does it just keep on going, stretching out into the void? I don't think I'll ever know the answer."

He paused for a moment to sip his tea. When Dad spoke again, his voice sounded small against the big sky. "The point is, the universe is full of wonders, Ryan. Some of them you'll be lucky enough to get an answer to, and some of them you never will. Sometimes you just have to accept that, and lie back and enjoy the view."

Dad's advice didn't make Ryan feel any better. He wasn't prepared to just lie back and accept that Clare's predictions were some big mystery that he'd never know the answer to.

A short while later, Ryan lay on his bed, curtains open, and gazed up at the waning Moon in the night sky. *Tonight was the night*, he thought. *Tonight was the actual anniversary of the Moon landing. It was exactly fifty years since the* Apollo *astronauts landed on the Moon.* He could see the Sea of Tranquility, where the capsule touched down. He imagined their bootprints, still there on the surface, stamped permanently in the lunar dust, for there was no atmosphere on the Moon, and no wind and rain to wash them away.

It was true, he thought. *Nothing is impossible*. But right now, he couldn't see how it was possible to contact Clare. All the avenues seemed to have closed off.

Ryan drifted off to sleep – a hot, fitful slumber, where he tossed, turned and sweated. One thought kept rolling around in his mind as he dropped off – how could Clare possibly have known those things? How could she have known the names of the Mars rovers, about the heart shape on Pluto, and the roadster in space?

How?

And then, in the smallest hours of the night, under the watchful gaze of the Moon itself, Ryan had a dream …

CHAPTER 9

Ryan looked down, seeing his bare feet treading across flagstones. Still wearing his pyjamas, he wandered slowly among a crowd of people. It was as if he was not really a part of his body, as if he was just watching from inside his head.

The weather was warm and dry, but it was cloudy and there was no Moon. He could see that it was night-time and that he was in a square – a large square with fountains and statues and columns. It only took him a second to figure out where it was.

Trafalgar Square.

Except it was different. Different, at least, to the Trafalgar Square he remembered. At first, he couldn't quite figure out how.

The people cramming the square were all dressed strangely, as if they were from a different era. Women in shift dresses, men in suits and ties and with slicked-back hair, and policemen wearing old-fashioned helmets.

Everyone was crowded round a big screen that was set up at one end of the square. Flickering black and white images showed men talking in a studio. Ryan couldn't hear very well from where he was, but he could tell they were talking in that kind of clipped accent you used to get in the old days. The mood of the crowd was tense but hopeful.

Ryan glanced around at the square's surroundings – the shopfronts, the old-fashioned red buses, the cars parked along the road. And the huge neon 'BOVRIL' sign flashing from one of the rooftops. There could be no doubt about it. This really was a different era. This was Trafalgar Square from 1969, the night of the Moon landing. Ryan was actually here. It was a dream, of course. It had to be. Yet it was a vivid dream, so real, like no dream he'd ever had before. He couldn't help marvelling at what he saw. Couldn't help taking in

every single detail; the waft of the breeze, the smell of traffic fumes in the air, the cool smoothness of the flagstones under his feet. And the faces in the crowd. A woman with peroxide-blond hair and a lopsided smile. A man reading a newspaper, his stubby fingers discoloured by ink and nicotine. A woman slurping ice-cream, the white creamy drips splatting on the ground before her. Were all of these scenes really just a product of Ryan's own mind, his own imagination?

No one seemed to bat an eyelid at Ryan in his modern-day pyjamas. It was as if he was invisible, a ghost walking among them

As he made his way further and deeper into the press of bodies, the pictures on the big screen became clearer, and the clipped accents of the commentators in the studio became louder. Pushing through, he came at last to the very centre of the crowd and looked around.

And there she was. It had to be her – the dark bob of hair, the pale, serious face. She was even wearing the same jumper from the school photo. She was standing next to her father, right in the middle of the crowd, just as she had described, gripping her father's hand and staring up at the screen.

Clare.

CHAPTER 10

The whole thing might well have been just a dream, but he would speak to Clare anyway. Why not? It was his own dream and no one else's, so what was stopping him? What did dream Clare have to say about those predictions?

"Hello," he said, squeezing in beside her.

Clare glanced at him quickly. Surprise flashed across her face as she saw that he was only wearing pyjamas. Then she turned her body towards Ryan and stared at him full in the face. Clare glanced up at her father, but her father didn't bat an eyelid; he just kept gazing up at the screen. Finally, Clare turned back to him, puzzled. "But … you're wearing pyjamas …"

"It is the middle of the night," Ryan replied.

Clare cast her eye over Ryan's shoulder. "Where are your parents?"

"In their bed, sleeping." Which was true, and that was exactly where Ryan was too.

Clare's brow creased. She squeezed her father's hand and looked up at him, but still her father didn't take his gaze off the screen.

Clare turned her face back to Ryan, confused. "Who are you?"

"You sent me a letter," said Ryan.

Clare wobbled her head and shrugged her shoulders. "What letter?"

"In the time capsule. At school."

"But we're burying the time capsule on Monday. I haven't even written the letter yet."

"We dug it up yesterday," said Ryan.

Clare's brow creased even further. "Yesterday?"

Ryan spoke of the three predictions in Clare's letter,

spoke excitedly and at length about the probe, the Mars rovers and the roadster in space. "I want to know," he said. "How could you possibly have known those things?"

At that, Clare gave a kind of smile. "Isn't it obvious? You told me."

A wave of excitement broke through the crowd. Up on the big screen, grainy black and white images from the Moon showed Neil Armstrong in his spacesuit, slowly stepping off the ladder of his Moon lander and placing his foot on the surface.

And then his voice, sounding quite garbled over the intercom and the thousands of miles of deep space.

"That's one small step for a man, one giant leap for mankind."

The crowd erupted. With relief, with joy, with pride. People cheered, jumped up and down, hugged strangers. Ryan felt it too – yes, even though it was a dream – the excitement, the happiness; it flooded through his bones like electricity. How amazing that his dreaming brain could recreate this incredible moment, making it seem as if it was real.

He glanced at Clare and she glanced back at him, and they both grinned wide. She felt exactly the same as he did.

Clare looked up at her father again. Even now, the man's face remained still as he watched the flickering images of the man on the Moon – except for a single tear rolling down his cheek.

"Nothing is impossible," said Ryan.

"Pardon?" asked Clare, struggling to hear over the crowd, but Ryan had already turned away and was squeezing his way back through the throng. Something was drawing him home again.

Trafalgar Square was fading into the distance now – the old red buses and neon signs, the crowd and the big screen and its moment of history.

A dream is just a dream, he thought.

CHAPTER 11

Ryan sat up. It was morning. He flicked open the curtains. The sun was already streaming over the rooftops.

He couldn't get over the dream he'd just had, and how real it had all seemed. Sometimes he found that his dreams slipped away soon after he woke, like sand through his fingertips. He hated that, and didn't want it to happen again, not with this dream. He was determined to hold on to it, hold on to every single detail. And he wanted to tell someone about it, fast.

Ryan ran down the hall to his sister's room. Papers and books were piled up behind the door. Ryan had to push it open. Martha was up already. Again, she was on her laptop, chatting and sniggering with a girl with blond hair who was wearing a woolly sweater.

"Watch it, Ryan!" Martha snapped as the pile of books behind the door toppled over. "That's important! Now what is it? Can't you see, I'm hard at work here?"

"But you're on the computer talking to someone," replied Ryan.

Martha looked affronted. "That's Tatiana. She's helping me with my last assignment. It's lunchtime where she is."

Ryan shut the door then raced downstairs to find Dad.

He was in the garden, reclining on a bench and staring out at the garden thoughtfully.

"Dad!" he cried, startling him a bit as he raced out of the back door. "Wait till I tell you about the dream I had."

Ryan plonked himself down on the bench next to Dad and told him all about his encounter with Clare in Trafalgar Square. He even told him about the tiny details he remembered, like the tiny splatters of dripping ice-cream and the smooth feel of the flagstones under his bare feet. "It was like I was actually there, Dad!"

His father rubbed his chin. "Hmm, it doesn't surprise me. You've been living and breathing that letter for the last few days. You've been thinking about it a lot. And last night we found those photos online, of Trafalgar Square in 1969."

Dad turned to face Ryan and tapped his forefingers on Ryan's temples. "You see, your mind is like a sponge; it absorbs things. When you're asleep, your mind processes all the stuff it absorbs during the day. Sometimes that stuff plays out in your dreams – and that's why it seemed so realistic."

Ryan thought about this as he sat side by side with his father, soaking up the sun and staring out at the garden.

He came to the conclusion that Dad was probably right. Yet it didn't stop him thinking about it constantly for the rest of the day.

When he went to bed that night, he was half-expecting to have the same dream, or at least another one like it, but he never did.

Monday morning came. A new week, the last week at school before the holidays. Ryan felt himself putting the letter and Clare's predictions behind him, closing the door on it as his mind moved on to other things – not least the summer that stretched out ahead.

He barely thought about Clare at all as he wolfed down his breakfast, tucked in his shirt and raced out of the door. He vaulted the garden wall and sprinted to school.

As he dashed through the gates, he noticed that Mr Deegan wasn't there that morning, sweeping up outside the gates, which was a bit strange; he was usually there without fail. *Maybe he was sick*, he thought, as he raced inside and leaped up the stairs to his classroom.

Kayden was flicking through his football cards with a glum expression on his face.

"Why so sad?" asked Ryan. "It's nearly the summer holidays!"

"Yeah, but the football season is over," replied Kayden. "And besides, I'm moving to a new school, aren't I?"

"Ah, so you *are* gonna miss me then," Ryan said, nudging his arm. "Don't worry, I'll come and visit you."

Mrs Pace appeared at the door. Her cheeks were flushed, and she was smiling. "Class, I have a wonderful surprise for you," she said, and this caused everybody to go silent

and lean forward. "Remember when we opened the time capsule on Friday? We had tried to find class members from Class 6A from 1969 – but without success. Well, we had a wonderful and unexpected visitor this morning, because one of the classmates has come forward, and here they are ..."

Mrs Pace stepped out of the way, and a figure appeared at the door. The figure was a tall woman with a greying bob of hair. As soon as Ryan saw her face, pale and round and serious, he knew who it was.

Clare Smith herself had walked into his classroom.

CHAPTER 12

"That's your girl!" gasped Kayden.

The world seemed to freeze. Before Ryan knew it, he was rising to his feet, his chair scraping back. Then, as if in a dream, he heard it clattering to the floor behind him.

"Sit down, Ryan," said Mrs Pace, but it was a faraway voice, muffled by the blood pulsing in his head. Clare didn't notice.

As Ryan continued to stare, Mrs Pace turned more forcefully and raised her voice. "Ryan! Pick up your seat and sit down!" This time Clare glanced at him, but it was no more than a glance; it went straight through him. Ryan did as he was told and sat down.

Mrs Pace waved her hand towards the new arrival. "This is Ms Clare Smith. She was one of the students from the actual Class 6A who wrote the letters and buried the time capsule."

Mrs Pace smiled at Clare. "And you travelled all this way especially for us?"

"I flew in this morning." Clare spoke in a voice that was very different to the one Ryan had imagined: light and happy and confident, with an American twang. *Then again*, he thought, *she had lived a whole lifetime, she was not that young girl who wrote the letter in 1969.* "I only wish I'd been here when you opened the capsule. I'd forgotten about it, it was so long ago."

"How did you find out about it?" asked Mrs Pace.

"Someone got in touch with a friend of my older sister, who still lives in the area. A street sweeper, he said, but he didn't give a name." Ryan knew it had to be Mr Deegan that Clare was talking about. Mr Deegan really had thought about it. Somehow, he'd found a way to get a message to her.

Mrs Pace invited Clare to speak to the class. Over the next few minutes, as Clare talked, Ryan discovered that she had indeed moved to America soon after the capsule was buried. She'd wanted to be an astronaut but never quite made it, although she did go on to work for NASA as a systems programmer.

Ryan so wanted to speak to her, to ask her about the predictions in her letter, but he didn't get a chance. The headteacher soon arrived with the photographer from the local paper.

"Now, who had Ms Smith's letter?" asked Mrs Pace.

"Ryan!" cried Kayden, pointing his fingers up and down above Ryan's head. "It was Ryan!"

For the first time, Clare's eyes fixed on him properly. The woman tilted her head slightly and narrowed her eyes. Before Ryan could open his mouth, someone whisked him out from behind his desk and up to the front of the class. He was thrust in front of Clare. The letter she had written all those years ago was pushed under Ryan's nose. Ryan found himself standing right in front of her, gazing straight into her face, just like he had in his dream, wondering when he would get a chance to speak.

And then, the strangest thing happened.

Clare's eyes widened as she took Ryan in, and her face turned pale. She gasped.

Clare Smith looked like she'd just seen a ghost.

The next few moments were a blur of camera flashes and gabbling voices. The photographer moved Ryan so that he and Clare were standing side by side, facing the camera, so they could pose with the letter. Mrs Pace and Mr Ferris joined them. The teachers were smiling, but not Ryan. And, as he glanced up at Clare's face, he saw that she wasn't smiling either.

Clare hadn't lost that shocked expression. She kept looking down at him, staring at his face. Then another strange thing happened. Clare's brow creased. Creased in exactly the same way it had in his dream.

In his dream.

How could Ryan possibly have known that look? How, when all he'd ever seen of the real Clare before now was a grainy image in an old photo?

As the photographer finished off, he hoped he might now get a chance to ask Clare the questions he was dying to have answered. But the chance never came. It slipped out of his fingers like sand, like one of his dreams. In a flurry of chatter, Mrs Pace turned Ryan back towards his desk, and the headteacher led Clare out of the classroom door.

Clare was staring back at him. It was as if she, too, was dying to ask a question of Ryan, but she never got the chance either. As she left, Mrs Pace shut the door, then launched into one of her lessons.

Was that it, Ryan thought? Wasn't he ever going to get a chance to talk to the woman who wrote the letter? To ask her about the predictions? Ryan sat there, boiling with frustration, until the bell rang a few minutes later.

He scooted out, hoping he could track down Clare before she left the school. He veered around a corner on to a long corridor that was lined with lockers and benches. Sunlight streamed in from high windows. There, he found that he wouldn't have to track her down after all. And that he wasn't the only one seeking answers.

Clare's tall figure stood at the other end of the corridor, clutching her letter in one hand.

"Ryan?" she asked.

CHAPTER 13

They sat side by side on a bench in the playground.
Ryan and the girl from 1969, who was all grown up.
The sun's rays beat down while the other children
played around them. Nearby, and just out of earshot,
the man from the newspaper was interviewing Mr Ferris.
It wouldn't be long before they moved over here. Ryan
wouldn't have much time to get the answers he wanted.

Clare was still clutching the letter in her hands, staring
down at it in shock.

"For years, decades even, I completely forgot about the
time capsule, and about the letter I wrote," she said. "I
was too busy, too wrapped up in my work and my family.
It wasn't until I got that message from my sister … It was
only then that I remembered. I started thinking about
the day we buried the capsule, and the night of the
Apollo 11 landing. It all came rushing back."

"There's something I need to ask you," said Ryan, who
couldn't wait any longer. "Those predictions – the Mars
rovers, the Pluto probe, the roadster in space – how could
you possibly have known?"

"That's easy," said Clare. "But it's also the hardest thing to understand." She turned to look at Ryan full in the face, just the same way she had done in Ryan's dream. And then she smiled. "Because you told me, Ryan."

Ryan suddenly remembered the words Clare uttered in his dream, which were the exact same words she was uttering now. "I ... told you?"

"It was only while I was travelling here, when everything was rushing back into my head, that I started to think about those predictions I wrote down. *Spirit* and *Opportunity* really did come to Mars, and *New Horizons* did find a heart on Pluto, and then there was the roadster and Starman. You're right, how could I have known?"

"But I didn't come up with those predictions, you did," said Ryan.

"No," she replied. "Because that night, all those years ago, when my father took me to Trafalgar Square to see the Moon landing, I remember this boy. He appeared at my shoulder. It was so strange ... I mean, he was wearing pyjamas. He was the one who told me those predictions. I thought they were odd and a little bit funny, so I wrote them down." Clare leaned forward. "That boy was you, Ryan."

He gasped in disbelief, although somewhere, deep down, he already sensed that it was somehow the truth.

Clare continued, "As soon as I saw your face in the classroom it took me right back to that night. There's no mistake. It was definitely your face. I remember it like it was yesterday."

"No, it was a dream," he said. "I dreamed the whole thing. And there you were, in my dream, standing with your father right in the middle of Trafalgar Square, just like you said in your letter."

It was a dream, and yet – somehow – it wasn't. They sat for a moment, staring in wonder at the letter in Clare's hand, neither of them knowing what to make of it. "Are you saying I somehow time-travelled back to 1969?" he said eventually.

"Do you have another explanation?" Clare asked.

Ryan thought about it for a bit before shaking his head. He sensed it deep down inside. Somehow, some way, he really had gone back in time.

"And here's the thing," said Clare, holding up the letter. "If you did go back, then whose predictions are these? Are they mine or are they yours? Did you give them to me, or did I give them to you? Think about it."

Ryan did, but no matter how far he bent his mind he couldn't figure it out. "It's not possible," he said.

A flash of orange from the bushes on the other side of the fence caught his eye. Mr Deegan appeared, wearing his council vest. He smiled at Ryan, then raised his broom, as if in salute, and melted back into the bushes.

Clare shrugged. "Perhaps we'll never know. One thing's for sure though ..." The air filled with thunder as a jet engine split the blue sky far above them. "Something wonderful has happened."

CHAPTER 14

When Ryan arrived home that afternoon, he found Mum, Dad and Martha sitting around the kitchen table. Dad was fidgeting while Mum was drumming her fingers and looking up at him from under her eyelashes. Martha sat opposite Mum and Dad with her arms folded and a look of fearful expectation.

"Ah, Ryan, glad you're back," said Dad, laughing nervously. "Come and sit with us at the table."

"There's something we need to talk to you about," said Mum.

As Ryan pulled out a seat and sat down, he instantly thought about the other morning, when Mum and Dad had both been a bit distant. They'd been a bit distant all weekend in fact. What on earth could this be about?

Mum glanced at Dad, and he gave her a nod.

"We've got some news," said Mum, taking a deep breath. "I've been offered a job." She slipped a letter from where it was resting under her elbow. The same letter she'd held in her hands a few mornings before. Mum flipped it open.

"It's at a big university in America."

She paused for a moment, gazing from Ryan to Martha and then back again.

"It's a really good job," added Dad.

"Anyway," said Mum with a cough. "Your father and I thought about it long and hard over the weekend. I was thinking of taking it ..." She trailed off at the end of her sentence, leaving half a question mark hanging over the end.

"So, what are you saying?" asked Martha. "We're moving to America?"

Mum nodded, almost apologetically, then Dad cut in. "We'd like to, but it also depends on you two, and what you think."

Martha blinked, then unfolded her arms and relaxed her shoulders. "Oh, is that all? I thought it was something serious." She got up and wandered over to the fridge, humming.

"You're okay with it?" Dad asked Martha, surprised.

She yanked the fridge door open, nodding. "Yeah, no problem. I've nearly finished my degree, I'll come with you."

Ryan wasn't surprised. Martha's friends were all over the world. In this day and age, why would it matter where she lived?

Mum and Dad turned their gaze to Ryan. "And you?"

Ryan searched his feelings. It was no small thing. It meant he would be leaving school, just like Kayden. He'd be leaving his friends behind, his home, everything he knew. It would be hard, it would be sad. And yet …

Ryan felt no big well of sadness inside. Quite the opposite. His stomach was tingling with excitement. He would be going to live in America, just like Clare did with her parents after the Moon landing. How great would that be? A new town, a new school and new friends.

Ryan smiled. "Okay, I'm in."

Mum and Dad's faces lit up. "Really?" asked Dad. "You're really okay with it?"

"We've been worried sick how you'd take it," added Mum with relief. "If only we'd known you would react this way, we would have told you last week."

"If only we had a time machine," joked Dad. "We'd have saved ourselves all the worry."

If only, thought Ryan.

Back in his room, Ryan leaned out of the window, and the whole world seemed new and fresh and different. The sound of thunder again, crossing the skies above, and he stared up at the tiny jet passing overhead. Its tiny capsule glinting in the sun, full of people heading off somewhere exotic, to new places and new things. Soon, he would be one of them. Soon, he and his family would be off on their own great adventure.

Ryan thought long and hard about Clare, and about letters and news, and about predictions. Would his new adventure match the journey he'd taken into the past, back in dream-sleep to that magical starlit night when *Apollo 11* landed on the Moon? Who knew?

One thing was certain above all – Clare was right. After the events of 20th July 1969, nothing was impossible.

Now answer the questions ...

1 Where did Clare watch the Moon landings in 1969?

2 Why did Class 6A take 'pride of place' at the opening of the time capsule? What does the expression 'pride of place' mean (page 11)?

3 Can you explain why Mr Deegan was reluctant to attend the time capsule opening?

4 'Martha looked affronted.' Can you explain what the word 'affronted' means (page 50)?

5 Why was Ryan unable to discuss the class of 1969 with Miss Bradbury?

6 Give three examples of things Ryan sees in Chapter 9 that convince him that he is no longer in 2019.

7 Are Clare and Ryan's versions of what happened on the night of the Moon landings the same? Look back in the story for evidence to support your answer.

8 Have you read any other stories that have similar themes or deal with the topic of time travel in a similar way?